£ 11 99

The Hen House

Kimberly K. Schmidt

The Hen House

ADVENTURES AT GRAYSON FARM

Kimberly K. Schmidt

Illustrated by Marina Saumell

ISBN-13: **9781530064311**
ISBN-10: **1530064317**
Library of Congress Control Number: 2016902741
CreateSpace Independent Publishing Platform
North Charleston, South Carolina

Published by Barnyard Press, USA

Visit us at www.kimberlykbooks.com

Illustrated by Marina Saumell
www.marimell.com

To my sons, Taylor and Parker: my first audience and my best critics.

Table of Contents

Fox Den

Big Barn

Farmhouse

GRAYSON FARM

Mare Barn

Hen House

N

CHAPTER 1
Run! Run!

~

"Run! Run!" urged Sergeant Pepper, the large black-and-white speckled rooster, as he crowed a warning to his hens. A slight movement caught his eye, as a red bushy tail disappeared around the corner of the barn. "Red is sneaking behind the big barn! Run for cover! Be sharp about it!" Pepper flew to the top of the white board fence overlooking the barnyard. From there, he could better watch for the fox and give orders to his hens.

"Oh my! Oh my!" The hens scattered, looking for a place to hide.

"No panicking, now! Keep order." He spoke as if the hens were his troops. "Order and discipline. That's better. Keep your minds clear. Now, all of you go find a good hiding place."

Some ran through the open door of the henhouse, feeling safe within the darkness. Two young hens peered out from behind the large knobby tires of the big green tractor, hoping they would not be spotted.

"Here, Goldie! Come here," Penny, the bright red hen, called out to her friend. "That fox will see your gold feathers for sure. Come into the mare barn with me. It's safe in here. Hurry!"

The two horse barns at Grayson Farm faced each other across a cobblestone barnyard. The show horses lived in the big barn with a wide center aisle and a hayloft up above. The smaller barn was for broodmares only. Those stalls were extra roomy and bedded in deep straw, ready and waiting for the spring foals. Both barns made good hiding places. The chickens knew a fox wouldn't go into a barn in broad daylight, because dogs and people might be inside.

"Come on, ladies! Be quick about it. Use your wings, for heaven's sake!" Pepper said. He exercised every day, marching about, so he was muscular and fit. He shook his head at the plump hens who were slow and out of shape.

The large hens were not built for speed. They stretched their necks out, legs pumping and wings flapping, and ran for their lives. Most of them were too heavy to fly very high off the ground, so they looked for hiding places behind and under things.

"Now where is Freckles?" Sergeant Pepper muttered, looking around for the medium-sized plain white hen. "That independent streak of hers is going to get her caught by a fox one of these days."

"Here I am," called a sassy voice. "Up here!"

"Oh, there you are, Freckles," Pepper said, relieved. "I'm glad you can fly." He admired the athletic hen looking down from the open hay-loft. "But you really should stay closer, my dear.

It worries me how you wander so far from the flock. Someday I may not be able to warn you," scolded the kindly rooster.

"That silly old fox can't reach me up here," Freckles said.

She had been exploring the grassy paddock on the far side of the barnyard when she heard the alarm and flew into the hayloft. She fluffed and preened her feathers, not in the least upset by the commotion in the barnyard below.

"Look at those fat hens trying to run." Freckles laughed. "Ha! They think they are better than me, but just look at them. Their wings can't even lift their bodies off the ground. Pathetic!"

Freckles watched from high above the barn-yard as all the hens found safe places to hide under Sergeant Pepper's directions. This time the hens had escaped, but if they didn't improve their flying skills, someone was sure to get caught. Freckles could fly surprisingly well, and the other hens could not. But flying was the only thing Freckles could do better than them. And they never let her forget it. She ducked her head as her laughter melted into sadness.

CHAPTER 2

The Hens

~

"LOOK AT MY EGG," SAID Ginger, shyly. "It's large and a lovely brown color, don't you think?" Ginger was a pretty hen, the color of caramel, with white lacey feathers around her neck.

The flock of hens gathered around the nesting box, bobbing their heads and clucking in agreement.

"It certainly is a most unusually large and lovely egg and the nicest warm-brown color I have ever seen," assured Goldie.

"I never miss a day myself," Penny boasted. "Mrs. Little can count on me."

"I'm sure it's lovely," said Queenie, barely looking up from preening her beautiful black feathers so they gleamed. "Mine are always the biggest, but I am sure it's fine, dear."

The hens all knew that Mrs. Little counted on each of them for one egg every day to take to the farmers' market on Saturday. The large brown ones sold the best. In spite of the fact that Freckles' eggs were small and white, Mrs. Little had a special place in her heart for the plain white hen.

"It's like she's almost human!" Petite Mrs. Little laughed as she pulled off her oversized barn jacket, shook her floppy hat, and told her husband about Freckles's latest antics. "Today, she hurried up to me and stopped just short of colliding into me. She leaned way back to get a better look, cocked her head, and looked me right in the eye. She obviously had something very important she wanted to say. I'm sure she winked at me before going about her business, strutting off to explore the barnyard and do who knows what. Sometimes I think that chicken may start talking to me one of these days!"

~

There were many chickens on Grayson Farm. Freckles was called Freckles because she had a few black specks in her otherwise perfectly white feathers. She was very ordinary and did not stand out in any way.

All the other chickens were purebred chickens. Most were large laying hens. There were gleaming black ones, bright coppery-red ones, and black-and-white speckled ones. And each of them laid large brown eggs. Then there were the fancy hens that were simply beautiful to look at. These were the show chickens that lived in a separate chicken coop. Some had rock-star hairdos, some had frizzled feathers all over, and others had feathers on their feet.

But Freckles was not fancy. She did not lay large brown eggs, nor was she particularly special to look at. She was just a plain white hen with a few black freckles.

~

"Here she comes, girls," clucked Queenie. "Here comes that odd Freckles. Pretend you don't see her. Maybe she'll leave."

Penny moved closer to Queenie. Ginger hesitated as she looked over her shoulder at Freckles.

"I don't need you anyway," Freckles said. "I have better things to do than gossip with you." All of the hens turned their backs and moved away, leaving Freckles standing alone.

CHAPTER 3

Freckles' Adventures

~

FRECKLES LIKED TO EXPLORE AND wasn't afraid of anything, which was unusual behavior for a chicken. She especially loved to go for rides. Mrs. Little had gotten a call more than once when someone had left Grayson Farm after a riding lesson and found a stowaway white hen in their truck or horse trailer.

"Hello, Mrs. Little!" Gary, the farrier, said one evening when he called her on the phone. "That crazy white hen of yours was in my truck when I got home from shoeing your horses. She even laid an egg right inside my toolbox! Like she didn't want me to miss it. Like it was a gift or something. Crazy hen! I've never seen anything like her. By the way, do you want her back? She can just stay here and live with my chickens if you'd like."

"No, she definitely cannot live there!" Mrs. Little was a small woman, but feisty. And she loved her chickens. "Of course I want Freckles back! You need to catch her and bring her home the next time you come out this way."

"Oh, all right," Gary said, sounding a little grumpy. "It's not always easy to catch a chicken that doesn't want to be caught, you know," he muttered under his breath. "It may take me a day or two, but I'll bring her back."

One week later, Gary kept his word, and Freckles was on her way home in the front seat of his truck. Freckles pressed her face against the window for the entire ride, staring at all the sights passing by. She saw a herd of black cows with white stripes around their middles and some creamy white sheep with newborn lambs. Next, she saw small goats leaping and butting heads with one another as they played.

"Oh my! I wonder what those beautiful birds are?" Freckles clucked as they whizzed past several unusual creatures in a pen.

The large birds had long, thin necks with crests on top of their heads and tall green-and-blue tail feathers. One of the birds had spread its tail in a wide fan of extravagant colors as it strutted around in front of the others. Freckles had never seen anything so beautiful in her life. Her eyes opened wide in amazement.

Gary drove the truck across a narrow bridge over rushing water. Below it, people stood on the shore holding sticks with lines dangling into the stream.

"How curious," thought Freckles.

They passed through a small town on the way, and Freckles, being a country chicken, had never seen so many cars all in one place before. In the middle of the town was a light hanging above them that changed from green to yellow to red. It was a beautiful thing to see.

Before long, Gary turned into the barnyard at Grayson Farm and opened the door for the returning wanderer. Freckles paused for a moment in the open doorway, looking around with her head held high, before hopping out, secretly hoping the other hens saw her arrival.

That night in the henhouse, as all the chickens settled on their perches, Freckles couldn't hold it in any longer. "Let me tell you what I saw today!" Pepper had already heard about her adventure but turned to her politely, happy to hear about it again. The hens did not look her way.

"We're tired, Freckles. Tell us some other time," Queenie replied, yawning. "Why you would ever want to leave the safety of the barnyard is beyond me." They tucked their heads under their wings and quickly fell asleep.

Freckles scooted slowly over to the far end of the perch, turned to face the wall, and squeezed her eyes shut.

CHAPTER 4

Worms and Grubs and Other Yummy Treats

～

EVERY MORNING PEPPER AWOKE WITH the sun. "Cock-a-doodle-doo! It's morning. Time to wake up!" announced the handsome rooster. "Here comes Mrs. Little to let us out. Wake up, ladies!"

Goldie yawned and stretched her wings over her back. She stretched her legs, one at a time behind her. She fluffed her golden feathers and shook the sleep out of her head. She clicked her beak, ready for breakfast. Eating was Goldie's favorite thing to do.

"Oh!" exclaimed Goldie. A slight movement had caught her eye. It was a tiny gray mouse with round black eyes and long twitching whiskers. He was hiding behind the metal corn feeder, sniffing and wiggling his nose as he searched for any leftover kernels.

Many mice lived under the henhouse. They had built an intricate network of tunnels under the chicken yard so they could sneak out to gather kernels of spilled corn and barley and then dash safely back down their hole. But it was dangerous for them. Chickens will eat small mice for a treat.

Other than Freckles, none of the other hens had noticed the trespassing mouse. Freckles watched with interest from her perch. Quick as a cat, Goldie made a dash and, before the other hens knew what had happened, she grabbed the mouse with her sharp beak.

The surprised hens, cackling, ran to share in the unexpected delicacy. Penny tried to pull the mouse out of Goldie's grasp. Ginger also, made a move to steal the treat away. Goldie turned and ducked her head, spinning to avoid the tasty treat from being stolen. Then she swallowed the mouse whole. The last thing they saw of that mouse was the tail disappearing down her gullet.

"Oh Goldie! You should have shared!" exclaimed Penny.

"Oh sure," said Goldie, "as if you would have shared with me. And besides, I was paying attention while you sleepyheads were still rubbing your eyes. After all, the early bird catches the worm!" she teased. "Or in this case," she said, laughing, "the mouse!"

"Come quickly!" called Sergeant Pepper. "Mr. Little is on the tractor and is pushing the manure pile. Look, we can get to the worms more easily. I see some big ones!"

The hens came running to his series of rapid clucks

"Yum!" said Goldie leading the way, waddling as she ran. Even though they were fed corn and barley every day, they loved the worms, bugs, and grubs that were hiding just beneath the surface in the manure pile the best. When the tractor stirred up the pile, it was a wonderful, wiggly feast!

CHAPTER 5

A Rooster's Job Is Never Done

~

PEPPER LIKED TO CROW. HE crowed practically all day long. It's true that roosters crow as soon as the sun comes up, but it's also true that a rooster will keep on crowing all day long just to let everyone know how great he thinks he is.

A rooster is a very proud bird, and Pepper was no exception. He was proud of his beautiful black-and-white feathers, his large size, his bright-red comb and wattle, and his tall and graceful curving tail. And he wanted the whole world to know it. So he crowed loudly and often.

"Cock-a-doodle-do!" crowed Pepper. "It is another beautiful day." The hens stayed close as they scratched and feasted on the bugs and grubs and worms buried in the warm manure pile. After they ate, they all sunbathed, thoroughly enjoying themselves.

"Queenie, come over here with me in the sun. I found a wonderful dusty place to get rid of these annoying itching mites." Queenie and Goldie lay on their sides in the sun, flapping their wings and fluffing their feathers until they were covered with dust.

"Ah, much better," Queenie said as she stood up and shook, a cloud of dust flying everywhere.

"Well, at least that Freckles isn't here, thank goodness. I don't like her," Penny said. "She's not pretty at all, and I think she's strange too. Let's go eat before she comes. That leaves more worms and grubs and bugs for us, anyway."

"Okay, if you think we should," said Ginger, ducking her pretty head and peering at Freckles as she moved away with the other hens.

 ∼

"Don't worry about those silly hens," Pepper said to Freckles, who had overheard them as they pecked in the dirt a short distance away. He and Freckles stood apart from the flock so he could keep a lookout for Red the fox and other predators. Freckles was the smartest of all the hens, so Pepper liked to spend time discussing things with her.

"I wish I could travel with you, Freckles, just one time. But I have to keep all of you hens safe from foxes and hawks and stray dogs. It's my job. I have to be on guard and stay at my post." Pepper stood straighter and puffed out his chest as he thought of his important job in the barnyard. "Tell me more about your travels. What is it really like? How big is it out there? Tell me exactly what you see," he said as he flopped onto his side, dusting his feathers and enjoying the warm afternoon sun.

"Well…" Freckles said. She got excited just thinking about everything she had seen on her adventures. "It's very big out there. But even on our farm, it's much bigger than just the barn-yard. There are deep woods and huge fields. There are two ponds, one large and one small, with wild geese and wild ducks swimming in them. Once, I even saw a beaver building a dam where a stream flows into the pond."

"Anything else?" asked Pepper with great interest, wanting to know everything.

"One day when I was riding on the hay wagon in the back field, I saw Red and Vixen and their family. I know exactly where their den is," Freckles said, fluffing her feathers proudly. "They had three kits this year."

This was important information for Pepper as the guardian of the barnyard.

"You must tell me more about that sometime. I want every detail." He was concerned to hear about the kits. That meant more mouths for Red to feed.

"Come now, I see Mrs. Little is coming with our dinner. It is time to gather everyone into the henhouse for the night," said Sergeant Pepper.

With a crow and a series of quick, loud clucks, Pepper called the hens to him. "Dinnertime, my darlings! The day is over, and dinner is coming—and I see we have table scraps today."

The hens came running as fast as they could to prepare for the night. All except Freckles, that is.

CHAPTER 6

Twelve Eggs

~

"NOT TONIGHT!" SHE CLUCKED SOFTLY to herself.

Freckles did not go with Pepper to the hen-house that night but instead ran over to the big horse barn. Freckles knew today was very important—the day she would start sitting on her eggs. She had been looking forward to this day for almost two weeks.

A chicken will lay one egg a day. Most of the hens laid their eggs in the nesting boxes in the henhouse, and the eggs were collected every morning. But Freckles liked to hide her eggs. She went into the hayloft, found a hiding spot where no one would find her nest, and laid her eggs there. Today she would lay her twelfth egg.

The other eggs had been lying dormant in her nest, most of them for many days. The chicks would not start to grow inside the eggs until Freckles began the long sit. The warmth of her body would begin the incubation, so all the eggs would hatch on the same day. Today was the day Freckles started sitting. Today was the twelfth day.

～

Once a hen starts to sit, it takes three weeks for the eggs to hatch. Freckles would have to go days without eating and drinking or dusting her feathers. Occasionally, when it was safe, she might slip away secretly and quickly get a bite to eat, a drink of water, and a quick feather dusting before rushing back to sit. It took a very patient hen to be a mother. Freckles was a very good sitting hen. When hens are good mothers, they are said to be *broody*. And Freckles was a very broody hen. She loved having chicks.

Most of the other hens had never had chicks. They never got to number twelve, and they were not smart enough to know how to hide them. Freckles knew that only one other hen knew about hiding eggs. That hen was Queenie. And Freckles knew exactly where she had hidden her nest.

CHAPTER 7

Queenie's Nest

~

QUEENIE WAS A VERY LARGE hen with luminous black feathers. Sometimes, when the sun shone on her in just the right way, deep-green feathers shimmered among the glossy black ones. She laid large brown eggs, and she liked to gossip and scratch with the rest of the flock. She was considered the most beautiful and most popular of all the hens. But she also knew Freckles's secret, and she had hidden eggs just like Freckles had done. Because Queenie was so popular, she got away with hiding her eggs, and the other hens didn't dare speak against her.

Queenie started sitting on her eggs the day before Freckles. Her hiding place was not as secure, but Queenie thought it would do. Her nest was in the mare barn, tucked in the corner behind a large wooden trunk full of horse blankets and brushes.

"Queenie, you need to lay your eggs in a safer place," Freckles said when she saw where the hen was laying. "Lots of animals can reach your eggs on the ground. Up higher is safer. Come with me. I'll show you."

"Humph," Queenie said indignantly. "You think you know so much. You mind your own business. I do not need your advice. My hiding place is just fine."

"Fine. Do what you want. They're your eggs," Freckles muttered, as she turned on her heels and walked away.

CHAPTER 8
Fox!

~

"I'M HUNGRY," RED GRUMBLED TO Vixen.

Red had a glossy copper-red coat. He was large by fox standards and very handsome. Vixen was his mate. She was smaller than Red and an unusual blond color. She was very proud of her beautiful brush—or tail—which had a white tip that looked like it had been dipped in milk.

"Well, then, go hunting!" Vixen stamped her dainty paw, tired of his complaining.

Normally, she would have helped with the hunting, but since she'd had the kits, she stayed close to their den in the briar thicket near the old oak tree.

"I saw two fat rabbits eating clover in the horses' field next to the fence just this morning. They'll make a fine meal. Go on, now! The children will wake from their nap soon, and they'll be hungry," she said to Red, who could be a bit lazy sometimes.

"All I ever do is hunt," he complained.

Red and Vixen needed more and more food for their growing kits. Vixen had three kits this year, and the playful, rambunctious youngsters seemed to always be hungry. Red knew rabbits were plentiful on the farm, and there were always field mice, but it was a lot of work to hunt. It took many mice and rabbits to feed all the hungry mouths in his family.

Besides, the chickens in the nearby barn-yard were so close. Red knew it would be much easier to get a nice fat hen to feed all his kits. He thought two hens would be even better. Two hens would feed the whole family, and he could take a day off from the task of hunting.

He licked his chops just thinking about it. Chicken was Red's favorite food.

Red knew it was nearly impossible to catch a chicken in the middle of the day. There were always people and dogs around. But he was hungry, and Vixen was impatient, so he decided to sneak through the woods behind the barn and give it a try. And then he heard them.

CHAPTER 9

Zack and Mack

~

"CAW, CAW!" ZACK AND MACK, the ever-watchful crows, had spotted the sneaking fox in the woods and sounded the alarm.

Zack and Mack were always on the watch for foxes, hawks, and other predators. They didn't miss anything.

"Fox! Fox! Right here below us. Look, look!" The loud crows cawed as they swooped and dove at the embarrassed fox.

"It's impossible to sneak up on anything with those darned crows making all that noise," Red grumbled to himself.

He continued walking along in a dignified manner, ignoring the tormenting crows, but it didn't take long to realize his plan wasn't going to work. Frustrated, he gave up and headed back towards the den.

"You can't get past us, Red! We'll see you every time," the crows jeered as they swooped at the retreating fox.

〜

Foxes are very smart animals by nature, and Red was a particularly smart fox. He knew the woman had built the henhouse to protect her chickens at night, and they weren't let out until people and dogs were around to watch them. The chickens knew not to wander far from the barnyard.

So Red came up with a plan. He was very patient. Every evening he crept down to the barnyard, keeping just out of sight, and watched as Mrs. Little put the chickens away. He knew them all by sight. He had been watching them for days now, waiting for a slip-up. And then it happened.

"Aha!" said Red. He pricked his ears as he watched the woman feed the chickens their dinner and then lock and secure the door behind her.

After checking one last time, she set out for the old farmhouse down the lane.

Red looked around carefully to make sure the barnyard was empty. He crept up for a closer look.

The henhouse was a solid wooden structure. It was painted red with white trim, just like all the farm buildings. It was warm and weatherproof inside, but there was a small, chicken-size opening that led to a yard that was surrounded by a wire fence. The wire was buried in the ground so that foxes and raccoons could not dig under it. The yard also had a roof to protect from climbing predators.

Red could see the chickens pecking around inside the fenced yard. It was early evening and not quite dark. The chickens were enjoying the last light of day when Sergeant Pepper spotted the fox.

"Fox, fox!" Pepper crowed a loud alarm.

The chickens cackled in distress and ran inside the henhouse. Pepper stayed where he was, watching, knowing the fox could not get to them in their yard. They were safe inside the secure enclosure.

But Red had seen what he needed to see. Two of the hens were missing.

"They must be sitting on eggs somewhere," he muttered to himself. All he had to do was find their hiding place and then take them home for dinner.

The house was too far from the barnyard for Mrs. Little to hear Pepper's alarm. Red knew it was clear to search the barnyard. This was his chance.

CHAPTER 10

Watch Out, Queenie!

~

FRECKLES HEARD PEPPER'S ALARM FROM the safety of the hayloft. She wasn't worried because she knew the fox couldn't get to her hiding place.

The big horse barn had heavy sliding doors that were closed every night. Inside the barn, next to Mrs. Little's office, was a closed door leading to the hayloft above. The only way into the hayloft was to fly.

Freckles knew Queenie was sitting in the smaller mare barn across the barnyard, behind the large wooden trunk. Freckles knew Queenie was not safe there on the ground.

"Snooty old thing." Freckles remembered how Queenie had refused her advice to come hide with her. "She'll be sorry she didn't listen to me."

But Freckles was worried just the same. She knew in her heart that Queenie's safety was more important to her than any silly argument they might have had—she was family, after all—and she knew that Queenie was too big and heavy to fly into the high hayloft, even if she had wanted to.

~

Queenie heard Pepper's alarm. She was frightened. She heard the soft, padding paws of Red searching, searching.

Queenie looked around for a plan of escape. She looked at the tall stack of straw bales used for bedding, leaning against the wall. But she knew she could not fly that high. She didn't see any obvious way out of her predicament, but she knew if she was going to leave, she had to do it now. Queenie hesitated, but it did not take her long to decide.

"No. That would mean leaving my eggs, and I won't do it." Her instinct was strong. Queenie refused to leave her eggs. But she was scared. Though she would not hesitate to attack a cat or dog that wandered too closely to her chicks, a fox was something else entirely.

She had made her decision. She would stay on her eggs and hope that Red did not find her.

Scratch, scratch.

The sound of Red pushing on the hinged door leading into the mare barn announced his exact location. Mrs. Little had latched the door, so it didn't open. Queenie held her breath and tried to flatten her body over her eggs.

Unlike the henhouse, the horse barns didn't have buried wire barriers to keep out foxes. Red saw a slight gap under the door. It wasn't wide enough for him to squeeze through, but it gave him an idea. He would dig.

Queenie heard Red digging. She hoped desperately some person would drive up in a car and scare him off. Or possibly, one of the dogs might come down to the barn. But she knew that was unlikely. In the evenings, the dogs liked to stay in the house with Mr. and Mrs. Little. Her heart was pounding.

Red dug and dug in the hard-packed earth. He knew he had to get in and out before morning.

～

The other hens had long forgotten about the fox and were safely roosting on their perches in the henhouse. Their heads were tucked under their wings, and they were fast asleep.

Sergeant Pepper had not forgotten about the fox, though. And Freckles most certainly had not forgotten as she strained to hear anything from the barnyard below. The hayloft was high off the ground and stacked full with hay bales, muffling any sounds. She couldn't hear the fox's scratching paws far below.

Dawn would be approaching soon.

~

Queenie watched the hole getting bigger and bigger. She hoped against hope that Red would not finish digging before Mrs. Little arrived.

"Ha-ha!" laughed Red at the frightened hen he could smell easily inside the barn.

He now had his head and shoulders under the door. He pushed with his hind legs and pulled with his front legs until his slim, agile body was almost through the hole he had dug.

He thought about how happy Vixen would be when he arrived with their breakfast. Chickens are a fox's favorite meal, after all.

And with one last shove, he was through.

CHAPTER 11

The Rescue

~

QUEENIE TREMBLED IN HER DARK hiding place.

Red followed his sharp nose. It wasn't hard to find Queenie. He couldn't see her yet, but he definitely smelled her.

"It won't be long now, my little dumpling!" Red licked his chops. Just thinking about the yummy, fat hen made him drool.

Queenie's thoughts were full of despair, as she was certain it was all over. Then, suddenly, Queenie heard a voice above her.

"Up here, Queenie! Look up here!"

Surprised by the voice, Queenie looked up and saw Freckles.

Freckles had flown from the hayloft across the barnyard. She looked down at Queenie from the rafters.

Freckles knew she had to think fast. The fox was only a few steps from Queenie. In a few short moments, he would surely see the hen and grab her with his big sharp teeth. Nobody would be able to help Queenie then. To be taken by a fox was every chicken's worst nightmare.

Quickly, Freckles took in the situation. The rafters were the safest place to be, but Queenie couldn't fly that high. Freckles looked around below her for another idea.

Rosie, the mare, was watching from her stall.

Freckles knew that Queenie could fly to the top of Rosie's door, but it wasn't high enough to be safe from the fox. It did give Freckles an idea, though!

"Quick, Queenie! You need to fly up to me, but you need to do it in two short flights," Freckles ordered. "Quickly, now! You can do this. Fly to the top of Rosie's stall door. Then, from there, you can fly up here next to me on the rafters," she said breathlessly, hopping from one foot to the other. "No time to waste. Red is almost there. Jump! Fly!"

Queenie hesitated, not wanting to leave her eggs.

"There you are, my little appetizer! I see you now." Red barely saw the black hen in the darkness as she pressed herself close to the ground behind the large wooden trunk. He gathered himself onto his well-muscled haunches and pounced, his jaws open for the easiest catch of the season.

Queenie burst into life. With her legs out in front of her, she lunged straight at Red for all she was worth. She flapped her wings in his face, cackled her loudest cackle, and scratched the surprised fox in the face with her sharp toe-nails. Then she jumped off her eggs and flew to the top of Rosie's stall door.

"Almost there," she whispered breathlessly. "One more jump!" Queenie jumped into the air, wings outspread, her eyes glued to Freckles and the safety of the rafters—but not before Red recovered from his surprise and leaped into the air, grabbing hold of Queenie's tail and one back leg.

"Oh no you don't," Red snarled with bared teeth, angry that he had almost lost this easy prey. He snatched Queenie in midflight and pulled her back to earth. "I've got you now!"

"It's all over!" Queenie squawked, grabbing the top of Rosie's door as she fell. She saw no way out of certain death.

But Freckles had not given up. She flew from the rafters and dropped like a rock. She tucked her feet under her belly and hit the top of the stack of straw bales with all the weight and strength she could muster.

The stack of straw bales started to teeter and tip over.

CHAPTER 12

Teamwork

~

"THERE'S NO POINT FIGHTING. YOU might as well give up!" Red laughed victoriously.

He gave one last pull on Queenie and dislodged the hen's hold on the stall door, but suddenly, the pile of straw bales came crashing down upon him. One bale hit him squarely on the head, and he lost his hold on the panicked black hen.

With a snort, Rosie caught Queenie's attention. "Quickly, dear. Grab hold of my mane, and I will help you up."

Spitting out tail feathers, Red worked his way out from under the remaining bales of straw. It wouldn't take him long When she tried to move, Queenie realized her leg was broken and she had a gash in her side.

"Quickly, dear." Rosie stretched her neck over her stall door; her long silvery mane hung down. "You can do this. You must try."

"Hurry, Queenie. No time to lose. Those bales won't hold Red for long." Freckles hopped from one foot to the other, clucking anxiously.

Queenie, shaking with terror, gathered all her strength and courage, and bearing the pain, jumped in the air. Flapping her wings, with her broken leg dangling, she managed to grab Rosie's mane with her beak and her one good leg.

Rosie winced as the sharp claws scratched her skin, but she held still. "Hold on, dear."

As Red shook himself loose from the last offending straw bale, he saw what was happening.

"You can't get away from me that easily!" Red said as he stood on his hind legs and prepared to snatch the hen from the horse's long mane.

"Oh, no you don't, you devil!" Rosie lifted her head and stepped back into her stall in one swift movement.

Red knew better than to jump into a horse's stall. Horses are big and strong and have hard hooves that could kick and stomp a fox to death.

Grumbling and humiliated, his stomach growling, Red didn't know what he was going to tell Vixen. It certainly wouldn't be the truth. How embarrassing! He had been outfoxed by a chicken and a horse. Red crawled out the way he had come, stuck his nose in the air, and trailing his long bushy tail behind him, stalked off with as much dignity as he could muster.

Rosie gently lowered Queenie into the wooden hay manger in the corner of her stall.

Queenie was exhausted and injured. She felt sad that she had left her eggs behind, but there was nothing she could do about that now. She lay still, barely conscious, in the soft bed of hay in Rosie's stall.

CHAPTER 13

Morning Discovery

~

Dawn was coming, and Freckles heard Mrs. Little speaking to Jake and Bella, the farm dogs, as they walked down the lane and headed toward the barnyard.

"Time to feed the horses, my beauties," Mrs. Little said to the pair of sleek black Dobermans as she scratched their silky ears.

Jake and Bella lifted their heads in unison and sniffed the air. Letting out angry woofs, they rushed to the freshly dug hole under the door of the mare barn. They sniffed excitedly with their hackles raised. Then they were off, running swiftly across the field, their noses to the ground.

"My goodness, but they are on the scent of something this morning!" Mrs. Little laughed as the frantic Freckles came rushing up to her, clucking. "Oh, there you are! I wondered where you had gone," said Mrs. Little. "Sitting on a nest somewhere, I assume." She smiled fondly at the broody hen.

Freckles had always been friendly and inquisitive, but something did not seem right to Mrs. Little.

Freckles planted herself firmly in the small woman's way and would not let her pass.

"My goodness, Freckles," said Mrs. Little. "What is the matter with you this morning?"

But Freckles would not stop her odd behavior. She kept hopping up and down and running toward the mare barn and then back to Mrs. Little.

Mrs. Little knew animals well, and she believed in watching their body language and listening to them. And that was why she listened to Freckles that morning.

"OK, Freckles, I'll follow you. What is going on?" Mrs. Little asked.

Freckles rushed into the mare barn and straight to Queenie's hiding place behind the wooden trunk.

The small woman followed Freckles. She knew her beautiful black hen had been sitting in this exact spot, but Queenie was gone, and the nest was crushed.

"What in the world happened here?" She looked around the barn at the ruined nest, freshly dug hole, and the fallen straw bales. "And where is Queenie?" she asked, though in her heart, she already knew.

Mrs. Little had lived on a farm long enough to know that farm animals were still a part of nature, and that wild animals would hunt to eat. She tried to protect her chickens as best she could, but this was not the first time that a wily fox had taken one of her hens.

"Now, now, Freckles, it will be all right. At least the rest of you are OK." Rosie had been trying to get Mrs. Little's attention by nickering and tossing her head up and down, her mane and forelock flopping.

"Not you too, Rosie! For heaven's sake! What is the matter with you?" said Mrs. Little.

CHAPTER 14
Rosie the Guardian

~

WHEN MRS. LITTLE WALKED CLOSER, the big gray mare gave her a gentle nudge with her muzzle.

"Are you all right?" She was worried by her behavior because Rosie was pregnant. Rosie had given Mrs. Little many beautiful babies over the years. She was soon due to give birth to a very special foal that Mrs. Little hoped would be her next show horse.

Mrs. Little quickly slipped into Rosie's stall to examine her. The ever-patient Rosie would have none of it. She gave the woman another push with her large head.

Before she knew what was happening, Mrs. Little was standing by the hay manger. "Queenie," she said in amazement, seeing the injured black hen. "You got away from the fox! How in the world did you do that?"

Looking into the liquid, dark-brown eyes of the gentle mare standing by her, she said, "I don't know how, but I have a good idea Rosie had something to do with it." She stroked the kindly horse.

"And I bet you did too, Freckles." She glanced at the agitated white hen. Shaking her head, Mrs. Little knew she would never really know what had happened in the barn that night.

She took off her sweatshirt and wrapped the injured hen in it. She found a cardboard box and bedded it with straw. Queenie winced when Mrs. Little picked her up and laid her gently inside. Queenie was still breathing and able to hold herself upright, but her eyes were closed from pain and exhaustion. Mrs. Little set the box carefully in the corner of the stall and ran to her office to make a phone call.

"Dr. Grover, I have a hen that appears to have been injured by a fox. I don't know how on earth she got away, but I will be there in five minutes." She spoke quickly, thankful once again that her vet had an office nearby, saving her the thirty-minute drive into town.

Mrs. Little rushed back to the barn. She reached for Queenie, but Freckles kept blocking her path.

"Freckles, what are you doing? This is no time to be silly. I need to take Queenie to see Dr.

Grover. Hopefully, she will be OK, but I have to go." Mrs. Little picked up the box with Queenie lying inside.

Freckles ran back and forth from Queenie's nest to Mrs. Little, obviously distraught.

"OK, but let's make this quick," Mrs. Little said as she set the box down carefully and followed Freckles back to the ruined nest.

Hopping up and down in excitement, Freckles looked at the nest and then back to Mrs. Little. Freckles could, after all, count to twelve. There were four eggs remaining. Freckles snapped her beak and stomped her foot impatiently.

"Oh look! Some of the eggs weren't broken," said Mrs. Little. "But Freckles, Queenie is too hurt to sit on these eggs. We will have to let this go.

Queenie is more important. Freckles, now, I really have to go," said the exasperated woman. She needed to get Queenie to the vet, but Freckles was insistent, and would not stop her unusual behavior. "All right, all right. You haven't steered me wrong yet, so be quick about it. What do you want?"

Finally having her full attention, Freckles rushed across the barnyard to the main barn and flew easily into the open hayloft door.

Mrs. Little ran into the barn and climbed the stairs two at a time. She met the impatient Freckles at the top of the stairs. "I'm here. Get on with it," she said, thinking to herself that she was crazy to be talking to a chicken.

Freckles ran to the corner in the hayloft and disappeared.

"Where did you go?" asked Mrs. Little.

Freckles peered out from a gap between two hay bales that had not been stacked as tightly as the others. The small woman climbed onto a stool and reached between the bales and found an opening that couldn't be seen from the outside. Just inside, the opening widened, and there was a nest full of warm eggs.

"Well, I'll be! I wondered where you had hidden your eggs. Oh, I get it! You want Queenie's eggs too. That's a great idea! Give me just a minute."

It took Mrs. Little no time at all to nestle the four large brown eggs safely among the twelve smaller white ones. Freckles had to lift her wings and stretch her body as wide as she possibly could to accommodate sixteen eggs. She was, after all, not a very large hen.

CHAPTER 15

The Surprise

~

THREE WEEKS LATER, MRS. LITTLE brought Queenie back from the vet. Her leg had been splinted and was healing nicely. The vet said she could come home as long as she was kept on restricted activity.

Mrs. Little planned on keeping Queenie with her in her office during the day, and then the hen could sleep in the henhouse at night with her friends. Dr. Grover had been worried about how depressed Queenie seemed to be, but Mrs. Little knew she would be happier at home.

The other hens ran to welcome Queenie home, and Rosie whinnied a greeting from her stall. Queenie was glad to be alive and thankful to Rosie and Freckles, but she was also sad because she had lost her babies.

"Just a minute, Queenie. I have a surprise for you. I think I know just what might cheer you up," Mrs. Little said as she carried Queenie to the stall next to Rosie's.

She opened the stall door and set Queenie gently inside. There was Freckles with twelve fluffy little yellow chicks.

"I'm happy for you, Freckles," said the black hen quietly to the smaller white one. It did make her feel a little better seeing the healthy little chicks all running around, scratching in the dirt, and hopping in the air to grab flies off the walls.

Freckles had spotted a big winged moth. She let out an excited, rapid clucking, and all the chicks came running toward her. The dutiful mother stepped back to allow the chicks to chase the bug and have a game of tag.

"You have taught them well," Queenie said, sighing.

Freckles took a step to the side as she looked over her shoulder. There was something that, in her sadness, Queenie had not seen. Four beautiful black chicks, larger than the others, were hiding shyly behind Freckles.

"Oh! Could it be?" Queenie was overwhelmed with gratitude when she realized what Freckles had done. She suddenly felt ashamed for how she had treated Freckles in the past.

"Come," said Freckles. "They have been waiting for you. I told them all about you—about how you were a hero and stayed with them until the end and then outfoxed the fox. Come, children, your mother is home!" Freckles clucked softly.

The four black chicks knew their mother instantly, but they were overcome with shyness. But, after all, she did look just like them. And they had heard all about her since they were first hatched. So they ran to Queenie and snuggled under her large, puffed-out breast. The cheeky one, Sammy, jumped onto her back for a ride.

Freckles laughed. "That one will be a handful."

Mrs. Little was watching with interest. "Well, it looks like you two are getting along just fine. I am surprised. I have never seen a hen give up her chicks to another. I guess there's always more to learn. Queenie, maybe you would rather stay in here with Freckles. And don't worry about Mr. Fox. That hole has been repaired and this stall is secure, with closed bars and a solid foundation. He can't get in here. And besides"—she stroked the silky neck of the watching mare— "Rosie will have a fit if a fox comes anywhere near her barn!" Mrs. Little laughed.

CHAPTER 16

Friends at Last

～

SPRING GAVE WAY TO EARLY summer. The chicks were growing up and learning to be on their own. They were becoming more and more independent from their mothers and soon ventured off as a group to explore the barnyard.

The chicks now had flight feathers and were old enough to fly to the top of the stall door to roost together at night. Some facing forward and some facing backward, they all snuggled closely together.

Queenie and Freckles, roosting side by side, kept watch from the rafters above. They were now best friends.

"When can we sleep in the henhouse with the grown-up hens and Sergeant Pepper?" asked Sammy eagerly. All the chicks admired the dignified rooster but were also a little afraid of him.

"Soon, my dears," Queenie assured them, chuckling. "You must wait until you are a bit older."

The other hens had learned what Freckles had done for Queenie, and they were also ashamed of their unkindness toward Freckles. They now understood that just because she was a little different, was no reason to dislike her.

"After all," Ginger said, "it doesn't matter that she is a plain white hen and a little smaller than us—or that her eggs are small and white."

They realized that some of them were red, some were speckled, some were black, and some were gold. They realized that they all were a little bit different from one another. And that was OK.

"So what if she likes to go for rides in trucks and horse trailers? After all, what do we know about that, anyway?" said Goldie, pecking happily in the dirt.

They all clucked and nodded in agreement.

Penny smiled. "I do just love the bedtime stories she tells of her adventures."

"Freckles is teaching me to count to twelve," Ginger admitted, ducking her pretty head shyly. She had always wanted to have her own chicks.

They were content as a group, and they all watched out for one another.

Freckles did learn to stay closer to the flock; she needed her growing chicks to learn proper barnyard etiquette. But sometimes Freckles couldn't help herself, and she just had to go on a road trip.

~

"Mrs. Little! She did it again!" Gary said over the phone one evening. "That crazy white hen of yours was in my truck again when I got home today. And this time, she had three of her friends with her!"

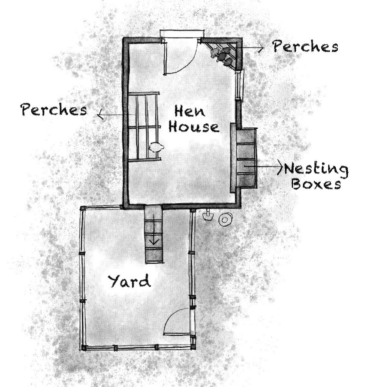

Perches

Perches

Hen
House

Nesting
Boxes

Yard

About the Author

~

KIMBERLY K. SCHMIDT IS A graduate of the University of Georgia, where she earned two bachelor's degrees—one in animal science and one in nursing.

Married with two sons, she currently lives on a farm near Charlottesville, Virginia, where she spends her time breeding and training horses and writing children's books.

Made in the USA
Charleston, SC
26 February 2017